Bradford Academy

Memorials of Rufus Anderson, D.D., Mrs. Harriet Newell

and Mrs. Ann H. Judson

Bradford Academy

Memorials of Rufus Anderson, D.D., Mrs. Harriet Newell
and Mrs. Ann H. Judson

ISBN/EAN: 9783337113209

Printed in Europe, USA, Canada, Australia, Japan

Cover: Foto ©Raphael Reischuk / pixelio.de

More available books at **www.hansebooks.com**

MEMORIALS

OF

RUFUS ANDERSON, D. D.,

MRS. HARRIET NEWELL.

AND

MRS. ANN H. JUDSON.

———

LAWRENCE, MASS.
AMERICAN PRINTING HOUSE.
1885

BRADFORD ACADEMY.

On Wednesday, March 26, 1884, the portraits of Dr. Anderson, Mrs. Newell and Mrs. Judson were formally presented
to Bradford Academy. The occasion called together a large
audience, including many distinguished friends of the school
from Boston and other leading cities and towns in New England. The portrait of Dr. Anderson, who was for many years
President of the Board of Trustees, was the gift of Mr. El-
bridge G. Wood and Mr. John L. Hobson, of Haverhill.
Mrs. Judson's portrait was given by the pupils of the Academy for the year 1883. The portrait of Harriet Newell was
given by Mrs. Mary F. Ames, of Haverhill, in behalf of the
Center Congregational Church in that city.

ADDRESS OF DR. SEELEY.

There are some duties from which one may shrink, though
it is very pleasant to perform them. Such a duty is that
now before me. I call it a "duty," because I perform it at
the request of two of my respected parishioners,* whose wish
(in such a matter,) has, for me, the force of law.

*Messrs. E. G. Wood, and J. L. Hobson.

As all present are aware, my part in these exercises, is the presentation (on behalf of the gentlemen referred to,) of this beautiful portrait of the Rev. Dr. Rufus Anderson, to the Trustees of this Academy, henceforth to occupy a prominent position in this spacious and elegant chapel.

I *shrink* from the service, because it could be performed so much more happily and profitably by others: and I am *pleased* to perform it, because, in the circumstances, the placing of this picture on its walls, is a high honor to this Academy, and is a fitting tribute of respect to him who was once a pupil, and of its late President. It is also a happy coincidence that the Institution is located in this good old town of Bradford, in which the American Board of Commissioners for Foreign Missions was formed, at a meeting of the Massachusetts General Conference, in June, 1813.

The Rev. Dr. Anderson was born Aug. 17, 1796, at North Yarmouth, Me., where his father, whose name he bore, was pastor of the 2nd Cong'l Church. In 1805, his father removed from North Yarmouth and became pastor of the Cong'l Church at Wenham; and, as Bradford Academy was then a school for both sexes, the young Anderson became one of its pupils. He entered Bowdoin College, (of which his father was a Trustee,) in 1814. By the students he was chosen President of the leading Literary Society, the highest honor they could give him; and after sustaining a high rank in his class, he graduated in 1818.

His father, like some other ministers of the Congregational Churches, had become deeply interested in the unevangelized nations; and the son, (being somewhat imbued with his father's sentiments,) chose for his graduating oration, the almost prophetic theme, "THE PROBABLE IMPROVEMENT OF THE WORLD."*

He then entered Andover Seminary, where circumstances gave shape to his future career. He here became especially

---

*A graduating oration on a kindred theme had been delivered by Rev. Samuel Nott at Union College in 1811, and Mr. Nott preached the first Missionary Sermon that same year at Worcester. He was also one of the first missionaries to India, whither he went in Feb., 1812.

intimate with William Goodell and Daniel Temple, two men who, like himself subsequently were distinguished for their labors in the cause of missions.[†]

When he had completed his second seminary year, he was invited by Mr. Jeremiah Evarts, Corresponding Secretary and Treasurer of the American Board, to assist him for a time in the missionary rooms in Boston, and he spent the vacation in so doing.

While in the midst of his studies of the third year, he received and accepted a similar invitation ; and as Mr. Evarts had to go south on account of his health, the Secretary's duties fell upon Mr. Anderson, who, nevertheless, after Mr. Evarts' return, went back to Andover and graduated with his class when he was 26 years of age. He now was appointed Assistant Secretary of the Board, and ten years subsequently became its Corresponding Secretary. This latter office he continued to hold for 34 years, when, after 44 years of continuous service, he concluded that the labors of his office should fall into younger and more vigorous hands.

He did not withdraw entirely from the cause which, for so long a time, had been the object of his thoughts, cares and anxieties, but occupied his closing years chiefly in occasional lectures, especially to young men in Theological Seminaries, in writing histories of missions (for which no one was better qualified) and in other literary work on behalf of the Board.

During these latter years, he was invited to take the Presidency of Bradford Academy, and from his knowledge of its early and subsequent connection with the cause of missions, and with the desire to promote more intimate relations between this institution and the great cause which lay so near

[†]We learn from a manuscript sketch of Dr. Anderson, by Rev. Dr. Dorus Clarke, that there was "at that time in the Seminary, a galaxy of foreign missionaries of greater number and splendor than perhaps has ever graced that beautiful hill, before or since. Among them, were such men as Jonas King, Hiram Bingham, Asa Thurston, Daniel Temple, William Goodell, Isaac Bird, and William Richards.

Dr. Clarke also informs us that "for some time during his residence at Andover, Dr. Anderson very seriously entertained the idea of devoting himself personally to the work of foreign missions, as a missionary in some foreign land."

his heart, he accepted : and to his influence in connection with that of other open handed and large hearted friends of this school is to be attributed the uprearing of these walls, the dedication of the building, free from debt, and the development of its scholastic character till it stands one of the foremost seminaries for young ladies in all the land.

Such is a simple statement of the facts in his career. If we consider the peculiar nature of his life work, its aims, its extent, the manner of its performance and the spirit with which he pursued it, we shall be convinced that he occupied a place among the foremost minds of his day and generation.

Like the statesman, it was his aim to act on his fellow men in such a manner as to improve their condition and their prospects. Like the *best* statesmen he rose above personal ambition and selfishness of every kind and degree. While the true statesman contemplates the welfare of his entire people,. occasionally some measure which he advocates, projects its benificent influence beyond the boundaries of his own land. But no mere statesman, not even the greatest, ever imagined it to be his proper aim to attempt the improvement of the entire human race. It was reserved for those who sustain and those who manage the affairs of the great missionary societies to adopt this aim, and into this work, which contemplates the intellectual, moral and religious improvement of all nations, all tribes, all of human kind, — it was the lot of our noble friend to enter.

When he became Assistant Secretary of the American Board in 1822, it had but 7 missions, the oldest of them having been established but eight years. It had but 24 ordained missionaries, and the receipts for the year were but sixty-one thousand (61.000) dollars. During Dr. Anderson's secretaryship, the seven missions increased to twenty. embracing *one hundred stations.* and two hundred and forty outstations, occupied by native helpers. A native ministry (which was first called into the service four years after he became Assistant Secretary) numbered at his resignation more than three hundred, of whom, more than sixty were pastors of churches. The mission churches numbered almost two hundred, and more than sixty thousand members had been received into these churches.

The receipts meanwhile had risen from sixty-one thousand dollars to five hundred and thirty-four thousand dollars per annum, when he resigned.

This however, is but a partial statement of what had been done. When he took the Secretary's office, the greater part of the heathen world, such as Western Asia, India, Burmah, China with their *six hundred* millions of souls were closed against missionary operations, but when he withdrew from office they were all accessible to the gospel. An immense preparation had also been made for the spiritual conquest of those countries in the knowledge gained of their populations and their languages, in the materials made ready for the warfare, in the varied missionary organizations in the skill and confidence which had been gained, and which are so needful in the conflict, and in the apprehension which so generally exists among the heathen themselves, that the missions are to be successful.

Such had been the progress of the American Board and other missionary societies, that Dr. Anderson at his resignation expressed himself as follows: "Never have I had stronger assurance than now of the ultimate triumph of the missionary cause. Its progress seems to me to be as certain as that of trade, or knowledge, or freedom of thought and action. With the world open to evangelical effort as it never was before, the truly evangelical churches will be less and less able to disregard the spiritually benighted nations."

Such is his story, and it is not too much to say that, considered in the highest and broadest sense, he occupies a lofty and honorable position among the most distinguished men whose names grace our national history. Best of all, he did not seek, and apparently did not think of gaining honor or fame, but solely of promoting the good of mankind and the glory of God.

It is well therefore that his portrait should be placed in this hall, that those who shall successively occupy these seats, as the years roll by, may be reminded of the man, of the great ends he sought in life — of the manner in which he achieved them — of his relations to and interest in this institution, and of his desire that its members should intelligently and heartily identify themselves with the cause to which his life was devoted — a cause which in the grandeur of its ideas, in the comprehensiveness of its aims, and in the radical and blessed nature of its effects, is the sublimest movement on the face of the earth.

ADDRESS OF DR. CROWELL.

"When'er a noble deed is wrought,
When'er is spoken a noble thought,
Our souls in glad surprise
To higher levels rise."

And our souls to-day, Mr. President, rise to higher levels under the inspiration of this sentiment of the poet. Seventy-two years ago, in the little village of Haverhill, on the other side of the Merrimack, a beautiful young woman, nineteen years of age, consecrated her life to the work of foreign missions. This determination so full of novelty, so tinged with the ideal of romantic adventure, was a mystery to her youthful companions, and many of the savants of the village shook their heads in grave doubt as to the results of an enterprise that promised so little. But Harriet Atwood had made up her mind to a high resolve. When she gave her life to the service of Christ in her conversion, it was no unmeaning ceremony. It meant anything and anywhere with the Divine Master for a leader, and He who came not to be

Mrs. Harriet Newell.

ministered unto, but to minister, and to give his life, was to her a complete pattern and guide.

In the ancestral home, and in the village church in Haverhill, she had learned the story of the cross. From that little band of devout and earnest men, gathered in the old meeting house at the foot of this hill she heard the cry of distress from far off lands; from the pious teachers of this time-honored Academy, she imbibed the missionary spirit; her purpose became strengthened, she joined her life with the life of Samuel Newell, and henceforth Harriet Newell stands before the world as one of the pioneers in the work of American foreign missions.

Companion-saint with her, who shares with thee,
The Christian wreath of immortality!

Among her private papers we find the following record, bearing date, Aug. 27, 1809: "When I entered my thirteenth year, I was sent by my parents to the Academy at Bradford. A revival of religion commenced in the neighborhood, which in a short time spread into the school. A large number of the young ladies were anxiously inquiring what they should do to inherit eternal life. I began to inquire what these things meant. My attention was solemnly called to the concerns of my immortal soul. My convictions were not as pungent and distressing as many have had, but they were of long continuance. It was more than three months before I was brought to cast my soul on the Saviour of sinners, and rely on Him for salvation. The ecstasies which many new born souls possess were not mine, but I was filled with a sweet peace, a heavenly calmness, which I never can describe. The character of Jesus appeared infinitely lovely, and I could say with the Psalmist, 'Whom have I in heaven but Thee, and there is none on earth I desire but Thee.'"

Under date of March 1, 1811, occurs this "Devotion," breathing the spirit of St. Augustine: "Father of lights, it is the office of Thy spirit to create holy exercises in the hearts of Thy creatures. Oh, may I enter upon this month with renewed resolutions to devote myself exclusively to Thee, that at its close I may not sigh over misspent hours."

And after she had decided to give her life to the work of foreign missions, in a letter to an intimate friend, just before she left her native land forever, she writes: "The glorious morn of the millennium hastens. With an eye of faith we pass the mountains that now obstruct the universal spread of the gospel, and behold with joy unspeakable the beginning of a cloudless day, the reign of peace and love. Shall we be content to live indolent, inactive lives, and not assist in the great revolution about to be effected in this world of sin? Let worldly ease be sacrificed; let a life of self-denial and hardships be welcome to us, if the cause of God may thereby be most promoted and sinners most likely to be saved."

Short, indeed, was her career. Within a twelvemonth she fell a victim to disease, and after many severe hardships, and much suffering, she found a grave in the distant Isle of France, before the work of her mission was hardly begun. From a worldly standpoint, her career would be accounted a failure. But, oh, what an impulse did her sweet young life give to the great cause of Christian missions! How did her example inspire faith and courage in many timid and doubting souls! How has her name come down through the generations as a talisman to every heroic Christian heart! How, under its glowing beauty, has woman given up the allurements of home and friends and joined the noble army whose banners now stream in every clime! Such a life is not in vain. It is perpetuated in a long line of faithful followers, whose paths "shine more and more unto the perfect day."

We have before us to-day, a touching illustration of the power of this young life in moulding and shaping Christian character. When the memoirs of Harriet Newell were published, shortly after her death, they fell into the hands of a young girl who was deeply impressed by the example of sacrifice and self-consecration set forth in the little volume.

Her life, too, was consecrated to the blessed work of ministration, presented to us, in beautiful symmetry, the dignity of true womanhood. This little book was fondly cherished by this devout woman, who, as the wife of the late Dr. Dorus Clarke, became eminent in that faithful band of Christian workers whose praise is in all the churches. Her daughter, Mrs. Hammond, of Boston, presents this precious souvenir to the library of this Academy, to be preserved among its choice treasures.

It is most fitting that Bradford Academy should recognize such a character as that of Harriet Newell, for it is but an outgrowth of the system of instruction that has marked the history of this school from its earliest inception to the present time. It is here that the great lesson of ministration and sacrifice has been persistently and faithfully taught. It is here where pious teachers have given a divine impulse to many a youthful heart that has borne the fruit of a noble life, not only in the higher places of the world, but also

> " In the calm and quiet ways
> Of unobtrusive goodness known."

And so, Mr. President, this graceful memorial which we present here to-day, has been furnished by one whose interest in this school has been unremitting ; whose early life came under the influence of its instruction, and whose services in later years as a member of the board of visitors have been highly valued by the Trustees. She gives it to this school in behalf of the Center Congregational Church in Haverhill, which has been for generations the religious home of an honored ancestry ; that church whose early annals, under another title, bore the name of Harriet Atwood. Receive it, sir, as a symbol of devotion to a high and holy principle. · May it take its place upon these walls beside the portraits of other notable characters whose fame has added dignity to this institution.

And as the pupils who are here before us to-day, and those who shall gather here in the coming years, look upon the girlish face, so faithfully delineated by the artist, and learn the touching story that it represents, may they receive the inspiration set forth by one of our poets, and say:

"Yet all may win the triumphs thou hast won,
Still flows the fount whose waters strengthen thee,
The victor's names are all too few to fill
Heaven's mighty roll ; the glorious armory
That ministered to thee, is open still!"

MR. PORTER'S ADDRESS.

MR. PRESIDENT AND FRIENDS:

The young ladies of the Academy, who present the portrait of Mrs. Judson, have assigned to me the honor of speaking in their behalf, with the request that some delineation of the life and character of this remarkable woman might be given on this occasion.

Ann Hasseltine Judson was the daughter of John and Rebecca Hasseltine, and was born in Bradford, Dec. 22, 1789, four years before Harriet Newell, and seven years before Rufus Anderson. It is interesting to remember that only a few weeks before her birth, General Washington passed through Haverhill and Bradford on his famous tour through New England in the first year of his administration as President of the United States.

Ann, or Nancy Hasseltine, as she was originally called, was one of seven children, and the youngest of four daughters. The sons died in youth or early manhood, but the daughters who were all educated at this Academy, lived to be distinguished women in the various stations in life to which they were called. The eldest, Rebecca, married the Rev. Joseph Emerson of Beverly, afterwards with his wife in charge of the well known school at Byfield, where Mary Lyon was trained. The second, Mary, was also a successful teacher, though preferring a retired life. Always the most delicate member of the family in health, she yet outlived them all, and was known to many of us as a highly accomplished and refined woman. The next in order was Abigail, the beloved and honored preceptress of this institution for many happy years, whose genial face looks down upon us from yonder portrait, as if in grateful recognition of the gifts which bring again to her side these beloved companions of her youth. The fourth was our subject, Ann, the brilliant girl, the noble woman, the devoted missionary, whose portrait is now unveiled before us.

Surely here is honor enough for one family! Four such daughters shed lustre upon the name of Hasseltine, upon the school which nurtured them, and upon the town which they delighted to call their home.

With the others, Ann passed her childhood on this hill under the inspiring influences of the natural features of the place which have since become dear to so many. She was one of the early pupils of the Academy, and was held in high esteem as a gifted and industrious scholar. Her associates found her an open-hearted, sincere and spirited companion, ever ready to engage in the recreations as well as in the studies of the school. One of her classmates speaks of her "cheerful countenance, her sweet smile, her happy disposition, her keen wit, her lively conduct," which made her a great favorite among her companions.

She says herself, in one of her private journals, that her life at this period was far too gay and careless; and her conscience reproached her for neglecting many duties which she had been taught to perform.

The first occasion of serious reflection appears to have been one Sunday morning, when she was about fifteen years of age. Just before going to church she accidentally took up Hannah More's work on Female Education, and the first words that caught her eye were: "*She that liveth in pleasure is dead while she liveth.*" These words, which were printed in italics, struck her, she says to the heart. She paused for a few moments, and felt that she would like to lead a different life, but then she thought that the words might not apply to her, and so she concluded to think no more about them. A few months later she read the Pilgrim's Progress, and became much interested in the story, so much so, indeed, that she resolved to begin a religious life; but various hindrances of a social nature intervened, and it was not until the next year, 1806, that she experienced that radical change of heart which brought her to the Savior's feet. I do not remember ever to have read a more thorough and convincing account of the emotions of the soul in turning to God than that which Miss Hasseltine has given in the pages of her journal, so full and so profound. Out of the darkness she came at last into the light, the light of the cross. Her torturing load of fears was gone, and gone forever; and she found peace and even rapture in the contemplation of the Savior who had taken away her sin.

The quality of her mind may be inferred from the character of the books which she read at this period with the greatest eagerness. The Scriptures, with such commentaries as Guise, Orton and Scott were her daily study; and Edwards, Hopkins, Bellamy and Doddridge, became her favorite authors.

On the 14th of September, 1806, she, with one of her sisters united with the church in this town, then under ministry of the Rev. Jonathan Allen. The other sisters joined the following year, a wide-spread interest in religion having been awakened under the earnest and helpful guidance of the principal, Mr. Burnham, a graduate of Dartmouth, and afterwards for nearly half a century, the honored pastor of the church in Pembroke, N. H.

After leaving the Academy, Miss Hasseltine became a teacher in Haverhill, Salem and Newbury, but the event which determined her future life was her meeting with Mr. Judson, during the sessions of the Massachusetts Association at Bradford, in June, 1810. Young Judson was a graduate of

Brown, and had already taught school and published two
text books, a grammar and an arithmetic. He was now in
the last year of his studies at Andover, and his mind had
become seriously occupied with a plan to carry the gospel to
the heathen. At that time there was no organization in this
country to support foreign missions, but the honor of insti-
tuting one fell upon Bradford at this memorable meeting of
the General Association, when in response to an appeal from
four of the Andover students — Judson, Nott, Mills and
Newell — an organization was effected which soon took the
name of the American Board of Commissioners for Foreign
Missions, a name which has since been carried into every
quarter of the globe with the banner of the cross unfurled
before the eyes of perishing millions.

The deliberations continued several days, during which the
members were the guests of the people of Bradford. Of
course the hospitable home of Deacon Hasseltine would receive its share; and we are not surprised to find Mr. Judson
there one day at dinner with some of the ministers. It is
related that the youngest daughter, Ann, was waiting on the
table, according to the old New England custom. Her attention was naturally drawn to the young student, whose
bold missionary projects were making such a stir; and his
attention, it seems, was somewhat diverted from his plate,
although the fair attendant little imagined that she had woven
her spell about his young heart, and that he was at that very
time composing a graceful sonnet in her praise. The acquaintance thus formed soon ripened into a mutual attach-
ment, and led to an offer of marriage. To decide this question must have been, with her, no easy matter, for it involved
the necessity of exile from home and country, and the proba-
bility of great sufferings in unknown lands beyond the sea.
We do not wonder that she hesitated. Her education, her
temperament, her social affinities, all qualified her to fill some
place of honor and usefulness at home. No missionary had
yet gone from this country into foreigns parts, and no woman

had thought of it, except perhaps Harriet Atwood, to whom the same grave question was at this time submitted. No one dared advise her to go, such were the uncertainties of the enterprise; and yet no one could persuade her to stay, so great was the fascination which the work had for her. It cannot be said that her decision was the result of a romantic or adventurous spirit, for both she and Mr. Judson had calmly and deliberately estimated the difficulties and perils that were before them. This appears in his manly letter to her parents, asking for their consent to the marriage. When the matter was finally decided, there was on her part no misgiving, no regret. "I am not only willing," she writes in her journal, "to spend my days among the heathen, in attempting to enlighten and save them, but I find much pleasure in the prospect. Yes I think I would rather go to India, notwithstanding the almost insurmountable difficulties in the way, than to stay at home and enjoy the comforts and luxuries of life.   *   *   *Behold the handmaid of the Lord: be it unto me according to thy word.*"

They were married on the 5th of February, 1812, by Mr. Allen, who also preached a sermon on the occasion, from John XI: 52, tenderly addressing the young missionaries as "my dear children" and closing the service with an original hymn of his own which was sung by the large congregation. The first stanza will show us the character of this interesting hymn: —

> Go, ye heralds of salvation;
> Go, and preach in heathen lands;
> Publish loud to every nation
> What the Lord of Life commands.
> Go, ye sisters, their companions,
> Soothe their cares, and wipe their tears,
> Angels shall in bright battalions
> Guide your steps and guard your fears.

Mr. Newell and Miss Atwood were present on this occasion, and were married four days later. On the 6th of February, the ordination took place in the Tabernacle Church at Salem, and on the 19th, Mr. and Mrs. Judson, and Mr. and Mrs. Newell embarked in the brig *Caravan*, bound for Calcutta.

Their chosen work was before them, beckoning them on with its animating promise; and their hearts were set upon it more and more, but the parting was an ordeal of peculiar sadness, because they expected never to return; "My heart bleeds" writes Mrs. Judson in her journal that night, after taking leave of her friends. "O, America, my native land, must I leave thee? must I leave my parents, my sisters and brother, my friends beloved, and all the scenes of my early youth? must I leave thee, Bradford, my dear native town, where I spent the pleasant years of childhood; where I learned to lisp the name of mother; where my infant mind first began to expand; where I first entered the field of science; where I learned the endearments of friendship, and tasted of all the happiness this world can afford; where I learned also to value a Saviour's blood, and to count all things but loss in comparison with the knowledge of Him.   *   *   *   * "Farewell, happy, happy scenes, but never, no, never to be forgotten."

After a voyage of four months, they arrived in Calcutta where they were cordially welcomed by Dr. Cary, who invited them to the English Baptist Mission at Serampore, a few miles up the river. While there, they were led to adopt Baptist principles, an event which providentially resulted in the establishment of the Burman Mission, and an appeal to the Baptist Churches in America to form an organization for the support of Foreign Missions. The policy of the East India Company was at that time hostile to missionary operations, and our friends were peremptorily ordered to leave the country. The Newells went first, and after many vexatious delays, the Judsons arrived at the Isle of France, only to receive the startling tidings of the death of Mrs. Newell a few weeks before. "O what news, what distressing news!" writes Mrs. Judson. "Harriet is dead. Harriet my dear friend, my earliest associate in the mission is no more. O death! *   *   * Could not this infant mission be shielded from thy shaft? But thou hast only executed the commission of a higher power.   *   *   *   Thou wast sent by a kind Father to release His child from toil and pain. Be still, then, my heart, and know that God hath done it."

The hostility of the government followed them here, and they sailed for Madras, where however, they were doomed to fresh disappointment; and finding no vessel bound for any other place, they took an unseaworthy craft for Rangoon, the chief port of Burmah, thirty miles from the sea, on one of the outlets of the Irrawaddy. The health of Mrs. Judson had suffered from such constant changes and hardships, so she was scarcely able to land. She was borne upon the shoulders of the natives, and as they passed along, crowds of people gathered from curiosity to see this strange looking white woman in European dress.

Here at last they found a resting place where they were permitted to stay. But their real difficulties were only just begun. How could they attempt to evangelize a people whose language they knew nothing of? And how were they to learn it? There was no grammar, no dictionary, and not even an interpreter to help them. But they had not come across the seas at such a sacrifice, and on such an errand to be thwarted by obstacles which courage and perseverance might overcome. And so they bravely grappled with the difficulty, and at last they conquered it. It took them three long years to do it, but they were rewarded for their pains an hundred fold in the oral message, the christian literature, and the sacred Scriptures which they were afterwards able to give the Empire of Burmah.

In 1815, their second child was born, and honored with the name of Roger Williams. Their first child slept beneath the waters of the Bay of Bengal, a victim of the intolerance of the East India Company which drove the missionaries away from the soil of India. And now after a short life of eight months, the little blue-eyed Roger sickened and died, and was buried in the garden of the mission. The wife of the Viceroy, hearing of the death of the child, came to pay its mother a visit of condolence, accompanied by her officers of state, and attendants, in all about two hundred persons. An opportunity was thus afforded, even by this sad bereavement, to cultivate a more intimate acquaintance with the Burman people. The Viceroy also showed a kindly spirit by sending the missionaries an elephant, occasionally, to accompany them in their excursions.

Mr. Judson commenced preaching in 1819, in a building erected for the purpose, called a Zayat. Shortly after, the first Burman convert was baptized, and a few months later, two others. Thus after a wearisome labor of six years in preparing the foundations, the first living stones were at last laid for the spiritual temple which was to be erected to the glory of God in that heathen land.

In all the work of the mission, Mrs. Judson was a genuine help-meet to her husband. She not only managed the domestic affairs of the home, but she taught the Burmese women and children, besides writing tracts, and assisting in the translation of the Bible, being herself an apt scholar in the language, and commanding her time with marvellous ability and wisdom.

These exhausting labors, however, proved too much for her health, and she was advised to visit India for a change. Mr. Judson accompanied her, and several months were spent at Serampore, where the kindness of friends, and the much-needed rest secured such beneficial results, that they returned to Rangoon with new hope. It was not long however, before they were both attacked by a violent fever, which left Mrs. Judson in such a precarious condition that it was deemed necessary for her to have an entire change of climate. Accordingly it was arranged that she should visit America ; and for this purpose she sailed for Calcutta, where some English friends offered her a free passage to England. The voyage proved advantageous, and on her arrival she was hospitably received in London, as the guest of Joseph Butterworth, Esq., M. P., at whose house she met many distinguished christians and philanthropists, including Wilberforce, Babington and Sumner, the chaplain to George IV, who had just come to the throne. She afterwards visited Cheltenham for the sake of the waters, and then accepted pressing invitations from friends in Scotland, to whom she became sincerely attached through their social courtesies and valuable gifts.

In August, 1822, she embarked for America, several Liverpool ladies defraying the expenses of her passage, and escorting her some distance out of port. She arrived in New York on the 25th of September, and proceeded first to Philadelphia to confer with the officers of the Missionary Society. She then came to Bradford, intending to pass the winter here ; but the excitement occasioned by visiting the scenes and friends of her childhood, and the constant demands upon her strength, added to the trying effect of the weather upon a constitution accustomed to a tropical climate, compelled her, after an experiment of six weeks, to change her purpose and spend the winter farther south. A brother of Mr. Judson was at that time a physician under the government, and station at Baltimore. By his advice she decided to locate in that city and take a systematic course of medical treatment. Excluding herself from society almost altogether, she followed with scrupulous care the orders of her physician, giving her leisure time to her extensive correspondence and to her preparation of a History of the Burman Mission, which was soon after published both in this country and England. Dr. Wayland, who made Mrs. Judson's acquaintance during her visit to the United States, has thus described her : " I do not remember ever to have met a more remarkable woman. To great clearness of intellect, large powers of comprehension, and intuitive female sagacity, * * she added that heroic disinterestedness which naturally loses all consciousness of self in the prosecution of a great object. These elements, however, were all held in reserve and were hidden from public view by a veil of unusual feminine delicacy. * * * When I saw her, her complexion bore that

sallow hue which commonly follows residence in the East
Indies. As she found herself among friends who were interested in the Burman Mission, her reserve melted away,
her eye kindled, every feature was lighted up with enthusi-
asm, and she was everywhere acknowledged to be one of the
most fascinating of women." It may not be generally known
that during her residence in Rangoon, Mrs. Judson adopted
the Burmese dress. Her figure, which was of medium weight
is said to have appeared much taller and more commanding
in the oriental costume, and her rich Spanish complexion
lent it an additional charm. Her dark curls were straight-
ened and drawn back from her forehead, and a fragrant
cocoa-blossom would often drop like a white plume from the
knot upon the crown. Her saffron vest, when thrown open
would reveal the folds of crimson beneath; and the rich silk
skirt, wrapped about her fine figure, parted at the ankle and
sloped gracefully back upon the floor.

It was during her visit in this country that the distinguished artist Rembrandt Peale painted her portrait, now in
possession of her niece, Miss Rebecca E. Hasseltine, of St.
Augustine, Florida, who has kindly consented to its removal
to Boston, in order that a copy for this institution might be
made by Miss Bartlett, whose success has delighted us all
to-day. The face of Mrs. Judson, as represented in this
portrait, is one which will not soon be forgotten, combining
as it does in an unusual degree, intelligence, character and
grace. We can understand the achievements of a woman
whose purpose is so evidently present in these animated features which have been so well caught and transmitted to us
upon the canvas. Nor is the picture any the less interesting
because of its quaint dress, and the accompanying palm leaf
fittingly inscribed with Burman characters. This Academy
is richer than ever, now that it has upon its walls such a
souvenir of such a woman.

Mrs. Judson sailed from Boston, June 21, 1823, for Calcutta and reached Rangoon early in December, to find that

war was threatened between Burmah and the Bengal government. Mr. Judson had made arrangements to remove his residence to Ava, the capital, a long distance up the river, and soon after the arrival of his wife, they set out for their new home, "not knowing the tl.ings that should befall them there." Home, indeed, it could hardly be called, for they found no house at Ava to shelter them from the burning sun by day, or the chilling dews at night. They had to remain in their boat until they could build for themselves a small cottage outside the town on the bank of the river. Here Mrs. Judson soon opened a school for girls, two of whom she named *Mary* and *Abby Hasseltine*, as they were to be partially supported with funds contributed by the Judson Association of Bradford Academy.

It was not long before the startling news came that the English had captured Rangoon with a large force and were advancing toward the Capital. Suspicion of treachery rested upon the few foreigners living at Ava and an order was issued for their arrest. Mr. Judson was seized at dinner, thrown upon the floor, bound with strong cords and dragged away to prison, in spite of the protestations and entreaties of his wife, who was compelled to remain in her house under a strong guard. At this juncture, she destroyed all her letters and journals, lest they might disclose facts which would be construed against her in the examination to which she was forced to submit. Hearing that her husband was confined in the 'death prison,' and heavily loaded with irons, she begged permission to visit him. This was for some time refused, but at last, through her persistent endeavors, she was allowed to go as far as the prison gate where she had a brief interview with him, only to learn of the horrors of the dungeon in which he was confined. And now all the resources of her heroic nature were taxed to their utmost to devise means for obtaining his release. She appealed to the Governor of the city to the Queen, to the jailers and other officials, but only obtained a few evasive promises, which served little else than to keep her from despair.

Day after day, and month after month, she went on foot two miles to the prison to carry some word of comfort, or article of food, returning alone, often late in the evening worn out with fatigue and anxiety. The only mitigation she could gain was the temporary removal of her husband to a bamboo hut in the prison yard, where she could minister to his necessities. "The acme of my distress," she wrote, "consisted in the awful uncertainty of our final fate. My prevailing opinion was that my husband would suffer violent death and that I should of course become a slave, and languish out a miserable though short existence, in the tyrannic hands of some unfeeling master."

But the worst was yet to come. When the hot season set in, the foul atmosphere of the prison was insupportable. Several of the prisoners died, and Mr. Judson was seized with a fever. Just then they were ordered away from Ava to another prison near Amarapoora. Stripped of nearly all their clothing, they were driven on foot without hat or shoes under the burning sun, until their backs were scorched and their feet blistered and bleeding. Mrs. Judson, on hearing of their departure, ran from street to street to learn in what direction they had gone. As soon as she ascertained, she appealed to the Governor for permission to follow, and started early the next morning carrying in her arms an infant child, born in the midst of these overwhelming sorrows. At nightfall she reached her husband and found him in chains, utterly helpless, and suffering from fever and wounds. Though exhausted herself, she summoned the feeble remnants of her strength, and hastened back to Ava to bring their medicine chest, which she had left behind in her flight. She returned with it only to fall fainting upon a mat, from which she did not rise for two months. In this extremity, she was unable to care for herself, her husband or her child, and they must all have perished had it not been for a faithful Bengali cook, who did everything in his power to minister to their wants.

Such, my friends, were the scenes of cruelty and terror

through which this brave-hearted Bradford woman was called to pass. Does history anywhere show us an instance of more intrepid, courage or unflinching devotion? Search the annals of Greek or Roman, mediæval or modern heroism, and you will find no name worthier to be honored upon your walls than hers. The late Mrs. Sigourney, herself one of American's noblest daughters, was so moved by the story of Mrs. Judson's life that she wrote some admirable lines in her honor, from which I make the following extract:

> " Tardy months pass by,
> And find her still intrepid at her post
> Of danger, and of disappointed hope.
> Stern sickness smote her, but she felt it not,
> Heeded it not, and still with tireless zeal
> Carried the hoarded morsel to her love;
> Dared the rude arrogance of savage power
> To plead for him; and bade his dungeon glow
> With her fair brow, as erst the angel's smile
> Aroused imprisoned Peter, when his hands,
> Loos'd from their chains, were lifted high in praise."

As the victorious English forces under Sir Archibald Campbell, approached the Capital, it became evident that terms of peace must be made at once, or the city would fall into their hands. Accordingly a royal embassy was sent to the camp with Mr. Judson as interpreter. The negotiations finally succeeded, and the war which had continued nearly two years, was terminated by the Treaty of Yantabo, February 24, 1826.

Arrangements were at once made by the British commander, for the safety of Mr. and Mrs. Judson and their little daughter Maria, who were kindly received at his headquarters and provided with a comfortable passage to Rangoon on a gun boat. Soon after, they removed to Amherst, a new town at the mouth of the Salwen, named in honor of the Governor General of India. Here they were able to rest in peace, with the prospect of an interesting missionary work under the protection of the British flag. But, alas! for human hopes. In a few months, Mrs. Judson was seized with a violent fever which her enfeebled constitution was unable to resist, and she breathed her last on the 24th of October,

1826, at the early age of thirty-seven years. She was buried near her home, under a large hopia tree, on a beautiful green bluff overlooking the sea; and not long after, her little Maria was placed by her side.

Thus ended one of the noblest lives ever consecrated to the cause of missions. To Mrs. Judson, with her husband, was assigned the toil and the sacrifice, the joy and the sorrow of planting the Gospel in the Burman Empire. She was permitted to reap with him, the first precious fruits of that harvest which has since been counted by thousands of sheaves gathered into the garner of the Lord. All honor to them that sow in tears; they shall reap in joy.

To you, young ladies, and to those who come after you in this favored school of learning, we commit the memory of this lovely and devoted woman whose face in yonder portrait will not fail to inspire you to noble deeds when you remember her as the Bradford girl, the consecrated missionary and the renowned heroine of Ava.

BRADFORD ACADEMY,

BRADFORD, MASS.

Incorporated 1804.

Trustees.

Miss ANNIE E. JOHNSON,
PRINCIPAL.

Teachers and Lecturers.

Miss ANNIE E. JOHNSON,
Studies of the Senior Year.

Miss MARY E. MAGRATH,
Latin and Greek.

Miss MARY F. PINKERTON,
English Literature and Language.

Miss CAROLINE L. WHITE,
English Literature, and History.

Miss ALICE I. BROWN. S. B.,
Natural Sciences.

Miss MARIE KETTEMBEIL,
French and German.

Miss MARY C. BARSTOW,
Piano.

PROF. SAMUEL M. DOWNS,
Piano, Organ and Vocal Music.

Miss LUCY BELL,
Drawing and Painting.

Miss JENNIE E. IRESON,
Elocution and Gymnastics.

REV. JOHN LORD, LL.D.,
Lecturer on History.

PROF. CHAS. A. YOUNG, LL.D.
OF THE COLLEGE OF NEW JERSEY,
Lecturer on Astronomy.

MR. ARTHUR GILMAN,
Lecturer on Anglo Saxon Literature.

COURSE OF STUDY.

FIRST YEAR.

Latin, { Caesar or Nepos.
{ Latin Prose.

French, German or Music.

Mathematics, { Algebra.
{ Geometry.
{ Trigonometry.

English Literature.

Readings in Ancient and Mediaeval History.

Lectures on Physiology, Hygiene, and Botany.

English Prose Writing.

Weekly Lessons in Drawing.

SECOND YEAR.

Latin: Virgil and Cicero.

French, German or Music.

Chemistry: { Eliot and Storer's El. Manual and Cooke's Chemical.
{ Philosophy.

Mineralogy. Brush's Blowpipe Analysis.

Botany: Wood, Gray.

English Literature.

Readings in Modern History.

English Prose Writing.

Weekly Lessons in Drawing.

JUNIOR YEAR.

Latin, Greek, French or German.

Rhetoric: Seeley's English Lessons.

Logic: Jevons.

Physics.

Astronomy.

English Prose Writing.

Lectures on Comparative Zoölogy and Geology.

Readings in Shakespeare and other English Classics.

SENIOR YEAR.

Mental Science: Hopkins, Hamilton.
Moral Science: Alexander and Hopkins.
Natural Theology: Paley and Butler, Chalmers' Lectures.
Evidences of Christianity. Hopkins.
History of English Language: Lounsbury.
English Prose Writing.

Lectures. { History of Art.
{ History of Architecture.
{ Church History.

Lessons throughout the course in English Composition, Elocution and Vocal Music.

Private Lessons in Drawing, Painting and Music.

Familiar Lectures through the course in Physiology and the laws of life, illustrated by a choice collection of Models and Preparations of the human body, forming a very complete physiological cabinet.

The school is furnished with well selected apparatus for illustration of Physics and Chemistry, and each pupil has facilities for personal work in the Laboratory.

PREPARATORY COURSE.

The studies in the Preparatory Course are as follows: Arithmetic, with Metric System, Algebra, to Equations with two unknown qualities in Olney's Complete Algebra, or its equivalent. English Grammar, Allen and Greenough's Latin Grammar and Leighton's Latin Reader, Latin Prose in Leighton's Latin Lessons, Modern Geography and History of the United States.

SPECIAL COURSES.

For advanced pupils, who come for a less time than the regular course requires, Special Courses are arranged in those subjects which they are prepared to take.

COURSE OF STUDY IN THE BIBLE.

PURSUED DURING THE PAST YEAR.

For pupils of the First Year: From Joshua to II Kings.
For pupils of the Second Year: History of the Jews completed, and the Prophets.
For pupils of the Junior Year: Life of Christ.
For pupils of the Senior Year: Lives of St. Peter, St. Paul and St. John, and the Epistles.

COURSE IX ART.

Free instruction is given in Art, according to the following schedule. Advanced students pursue a higher course in Art study, for which there is extra charge:

FIRST YEAR.

FIRST TERM.

Freehand drawing, giving practice in straight and curved lines. Exercises drawn from dictation and memory.

SECOND TERM.

Drawings made in outline from flowers, leaves and other simple forms from nature. Natural forms conventionalized. Original designs made from conventional forms.

THIRD TERM.

Outline drawing from casts. Studies in foliage and architectural ornaments from engraved copies. Shading.

SECOND YEAR.

FIRST TERM.

Practice in straight and curved lines, conventional forms and designing. Drawing and shading from casts and other models.

SECOND TERM.

Studies made of the human figure from casts, and of landscapes, and animals from engraved copies. The last half of the term devoted to the study of Perspective.

THIRD TERM.

Studies in Perspective continued. Drawing and shading in charcoal from casts and other models, and from natural forms. Sketching from nature when practicable. Decorative work in pen, ink, and sepia.

COURSE IN MUSIC.

--

The course of study for the Piano Forte, embraces selections adapted to the requirements of the pupil, from the following authors:

Czerny, Cramer, Jensen, Krause, Loeschhorn, Bach's Inventions, Clementi's "Gradus ad Parnassum" (Tausig), Eschmann, Bennett, Moscheles, Bach's French and English Suites ; Grund, Harberbier (Poesies) Chopin, Henselt, Kullak's Octave Studies, Bach's "Well Tempered Clavier," Rubenstein, Raff, Brahms, Rheinberger, Beethoven, Mozart, Schumann, Mendelssohn, Saint Saens, Scarlatti, Handel, John Field and others.

In the study of Vocal Music, exercises, embracing a wide range in the Italian and English schools are used. Especial care is given to the manner of breathing, and its practical application to the formation of pure tones. The study of the diatonic scale is constant on the Italian vowels, and great attention is given to phrasing, and clear enunciation. The principal text-books in Harmony are Richter's Manual, and Emery's Harmony.

It is the aim of the teachers in this department, while developing the technical skill necessary for the modern school, to stimulate the musical sense, and cultivate a love for what is best and noblest in the art.

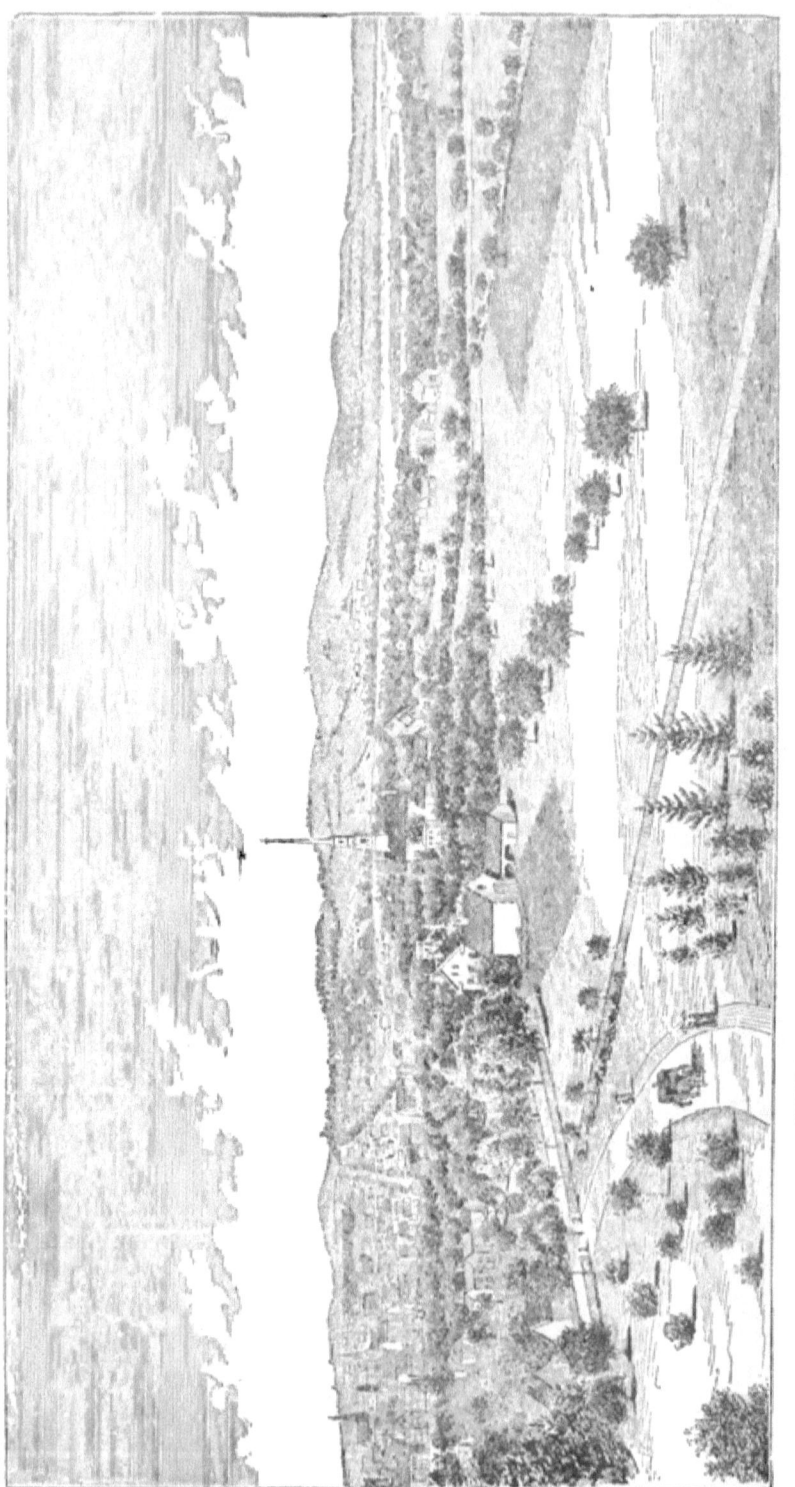

EASTERN VIEW OF THE VALLEY OF THE MERRIMACK, AS SEEN FROM BRADFORD ACADEMY.

CALENDAR.

THE YEAR 1885 86.

First Term opens . . . . TUESDAY, September 8, 1885
First Term closes . . . . WEDNESDAY, DEC. 2, 1885.
SECOND TERM opens . . . . TUESDAY, DEC. 8, 1885.
Recess at Christmas time.
SECOND TERM closes . . . . FRIDAY, March 5, 1886.
THIRD TERM opens . . . . TUESDAY, March 23, 1886.
THIRD TERM closes . . . . WEDNESDAY, June 23, 1886.

The academic year closes on the last Wednesday but one in June, and consists of three terms.

The year 1885-86 will commence on the second Tuesday in September.

EXPENSES.

BOARD, including washing, fuel and lights, FIRST TERM, . . . $80.00
"   "   "   "   "   SECOND TERM, . .   90.00
"   "   "   "   "   THIRD TERM, . . .   90.00
TUITION, including English branches, Latin and French, Greek or
German, and Vocal Music in Classes, ($20.00 per term), for
the year 60.00

Total expenses for the year, ...   320.00
Special rates to daughters of Clergymen and missionaries.
No extras except the following :
TUITION IN MUSIC AND ART :
Instruction on Piano, per term, ... $20.00 to $40.00
Use of Piano one hour a day, per term 3.00
Instruction in Art, including Linear and Perspective Drawing and
Painting, according to the ability of the pupil, per term, . . .   16.00

PARLOR OF A SUITE.

GENERAL INFORMATION.

Tuition and one-half the board must be paid during the *first* week of each term.

There will be no deduction in tuition for absence.

In case of protracted absence, one-half the board will be deducted during the time of absence.

There will be no charge for board to those pupils who remain at the Academy during the holiday recess, and no deduction for those who are absent. During vacation in March, five dollars a week will be charged to those pupils who remain.

Application may be made to Miss ANNIE E. JOHNSON, Principal. In case of a failure after an engagement has been made, information should be given immediately.

Applicants for admission are required to bring certificates of good moral standing from the principal of the school from which they come.

For admission to the regular course, an examination is required in Arithmetic, including the Metric System, Algebra to equations with two unknown quantities in Olney's Complete Algebra, or its equivalent, English Grammar, Latin Grammar, Latin Reader, Latin Prose in Leighton's Latin Lessons, Modern Geography, and History of the United States.

Pupils entering special courses must pass examinations in Preparatory Studies.

For admission to an advanced class, an examination is required in the preceding studies of the course, or their equivalents.

It is expected that pupils, whether entering in September, or later, will remain till the close of the school year.

Each pupil should be provided with towels and napkins, thick boots and overshoes, umbrella and waterproof, and have each article of her dress marked with her full name.

Books and stationery can be had at the institution.

Bradford is on the line of the Boston and Maine Railroad, thirty miles from Boston.

TUPELO LAKE (From the Bridge).

CIRCULAR.

BRADFORD ACADEMY is the oldest seminary for young ladies in the country. Founded in 1803, and incorporated in 1804, it has been in successful operation ever since. The school edifice, including the boarding and school departments under the same roof, is located near the centre of an area of twenty-five acres, twelve of which are covered with a fine growth of oaks, and are laid out with paths for exercise and recreation. The other portions of the grounds are under the charge of competent persons with a system of constant improvement to adorn the same with walks, shrubs, and trees, so as to give increased beauty and promote the comfort of those connected with the Academy. The situation is elevated, overlooking the city of Haverhill, across the River Merrimack, and commanding broad views on every side. The air is fresh and invigorating, and the healthfulness of the location has been abundantly proved during the past years of the school. The building is of brick, four stories high, in the form of a cross, wide corridors extending from east to west, and affording healthful promenades in inclement weather. A parlor and two bed-rooms constitute a suite of rooms for four pupils. These rooms are eleven and twelve feet high, and receive a full supply of air and sunlight. The school hall, recitation and music rooms, library, reading-rooms, parlors, dining-room, rooms for business, bathing-rooms, and closets, are all ordered on a generous scale for convenience, health and comfort. The entire building is heated by steam, and lighted by gas, and supplied with an abundance of pure water. No efforts are spared to make this a model establishment.

An addition to the west wing is now completed. It is 86 x 52 feet, three stories above the basement, and built of brick and granite. There are in it a bowling alley, gymnasium, laboratory, art room, twelve music rooms, and an observatory. There are elegant suites of rooms for the accommodation of twenty more pupils. The finely constructed flight of stairs in the south end of the annex will furnish perfect and ample fire escape for the whole academy — when taken in connection with what there now is. The inside is finished in the best of western brown ash. This addition is designed to furnish such complete facilities as shall make Bradford Academy, in all its appointments, as perfect as possible.

The course of study has been recently revised and enlarged to meet the demands of the present day, and secure a thorough and broad mental development. The course is comprehensive, embracing both the solid and ornamental branches. Three full studies for each term are assigned to each pupil, and are considered sufficient, as the multiplication of subjects leads to superficial knowledge, rather than true growth of mind. Care has been taken to secure the best instruction in the various branches of study. Besides the regular teachers, lecturers of eminence in various departments are employed.

Rev. John Lord, LL.D. has been for many years connected with the school as a lecturer on history.

TUPELO LAKE (FROM THE LAWN).

Prof. Charles A. Young, LL.D., of The College of New Jersey, lectures on astronomy.

The Library has had large additions made to it recently, selected with great care from all departments of literature, furnishing works of the highest authority; and in the department of Art, works of great cost and beauty. The reading room is well supplied with current literature.

The natural-history room is furnished with a valuable cabinet of minerals, and a collection of shells and curiosities; and a physiological cabinet.

Neatness and simplicity of dress, and the maintenance of a sound physical condition, are enjoined upon all. Daily exercise in the open air is required when the weather permits; and a room has been recently fitted up with gymnastic apparatus adapted to the wants of the pupils in that regard.

There is also an opportunity for boating and skating upon Tupelo Lake, in "Academic Grove," connected with the institution.

The pupils are under the constant care of teachers whose earnest effort is to form their characters on the basis of Christian principle. The Bible is read daily, and made a study in the school, and all are required to attend public worship on the Sabbath.

It is the design of the Trustees to surround all the pupils who come to this Institution with the best of home influence; and it will ever be their care to enjoin upon those who are brought into immediate charge of pupils, to spare no pains in promoting their social and physical good.

THE LIBRARY.

The members of the school have free access to the Library under the charge of the Librarian. It contains nearly four thousand volumes, selected with special reference to the needs of the institution.

The following books have been added by donation during the past year:

From Hon. Eben F. Stone, M. C.

Report of 10th United States Census. 10 Vols.

From John Crowell, M. D.

Jeançon's "Atlas of Human Anatomy."

From Hon. Eben F. Stone, M. C.

Report of Smithsonian Institution.
Forest Trees of North America, with Maps.
Report on Finance, U. S.
Report of U. S. Geological Survey.

From Bureau of Education.

Educational Reports. 2 Vols.

From Hon. L. Emery, Jr.

Geology of State of Pennsylvania.
Small's Legislative Handbook of Pennsylvania.

From Mrs. S. D. Warren.

Drummond's Natural Laws in the Spiritual World.

From Dr. & Mrs. Allen.

Divine Origin of Christianity. By Dr. Storrs.